I SPY
OUTER SPACE

I SPY with my little eyes, something beginning with...

A is for

Astronaut

I SPY with my little eyes, something beginning with...

B

is for

Black hole

I SPY with my little eyes, something beginning with... C and D

C  is for

Comet

D is for

Haumea

Dwarf planet

I SPY with my little eyes, something beginning with...

E is for

Earth

I SPY with my little eyes, something beginning with...

F is for Flare

I SPY with my little eyes, something beginning with...

G and H

G is for

Galaxy

H is for

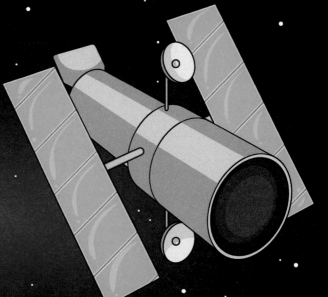

Hubble telescope

I SPY with my little eyes, something beginning with...

I is for

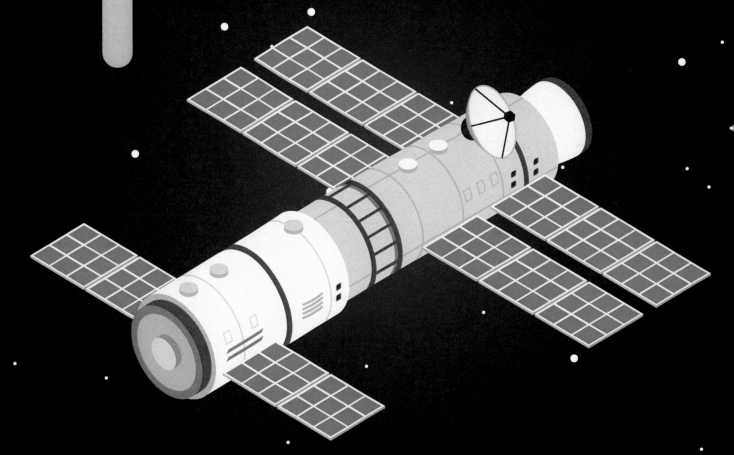

I.S.S.

I SPY with my little eyes, something beginning with...

I SPY with my little eyes, something beginning with...

K and L

Kuiper belt

K

is for

Kuiper belt

is for

L

Lander

I SPY with my little eyes, something beginning with...

M

I SPY with my little eyes, something beginning with...

N is for

Neptune

I SPY with my little eyes, something beginning with...

O and P

O is for

Observatory

P is for

Pluto

I SPY with my little eyes, something beginning with...

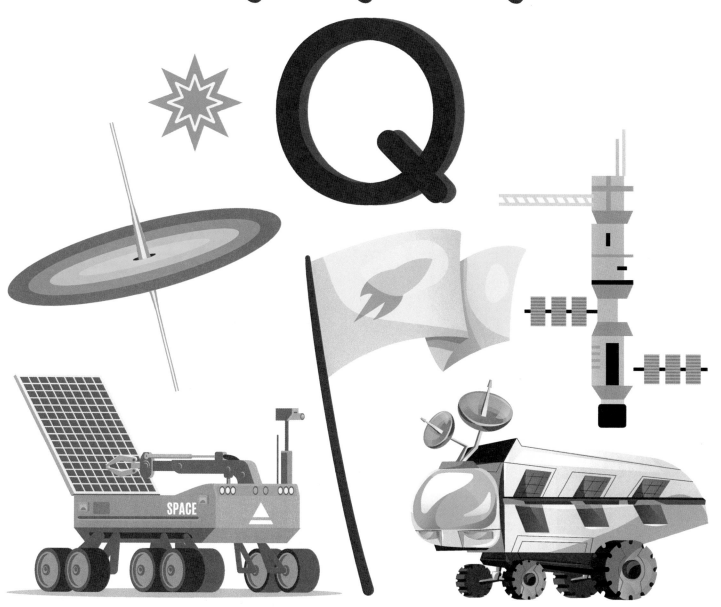

Q is for

Quasar

I SPY with my little eyes, something beginning with...

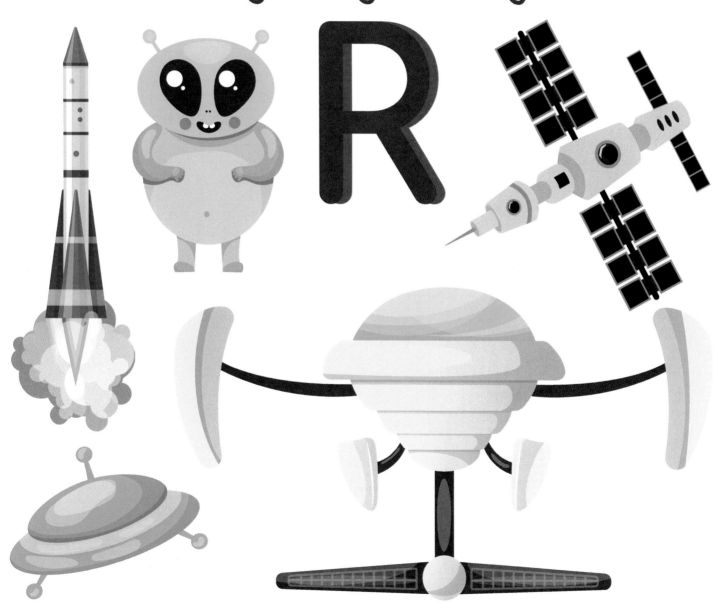

R is for

Rocket

I SPY with my little eyes, something beginning with...

S and T

S is for

Satellite

T is for

Telescope

I SPY with my little eyes, something beginning with...

I SPY with my little eyes, something beginning with...

V is for

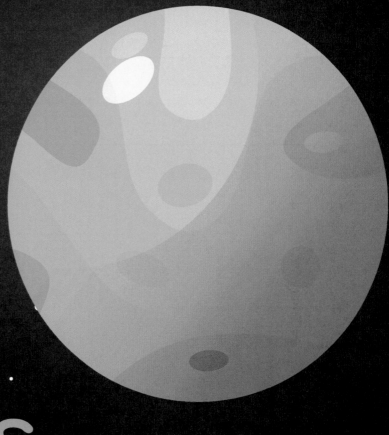

Venus

I SPY with my little eyes, something beginning with... W and X

W is for

White dwarf

X is for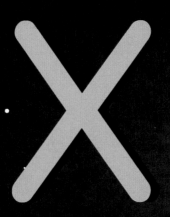

X-ray telescope

I SPY with my little eyes, something beginning with...

I SPY with my little eyes, something beginning with...

Z is for

Pisces

Aries

Taurus

Capricorn

Aquarius

Scorpio

Gemini

Cancer

Leo

Virgo

Libra

Sagittarius

Zodiac

Made in the USA
Monee, IL
25 March 2022

93527873R00026